June Bug on a String

Written By:
Rose Wilson

Illustrated By: Raquel Rodriguez

Library of Congress Control Number: 2016904830

ISBN: Softcover   9781514467664
        EBook   9781514467671

Print information available on the last page

Rev. date: 03/22/2016

To order additional copies of this book, contact:
Xlibris
1-888-795-4274
www.Xlibris.com
Orders@Xlibris.com

June Bug On A String

Once upon a summer day, in a neighborhood filled with children and play lives a six-year old girl named Rose Marie. She and her two brothers and eight sisters live in a two-story house on a busy street corner.

In the front yard, a forty-foot tall, Red Maple shade tree provides a canopy in the summer sun for romping and skipping on the lush, green grass.

Rose Marie hangs her suntanned body upside down by her knees from the lower branches of the tree. As she rocks back and forth, her long, blonde hair swishes in the wind.

At some point in the moment, she hears the jingling of the ice cream truck.

She twists down from the tree and watches as the deliciously painted mural of ice cream sandwiches, popsicles, and fudgesicles rolls by and stops at the corner.

Parents and children surround the merry arrival. Excitedly, each child waves a quarter in the air as they await their choice and purchase from a pleasing assortment.

Rose Marie knows Momma will not have a spare quarter for a frozen treat. She skips around the tree and whistles a tune.

Saturday of the following week rolls around and Rose Marie is in the kitchen helping Momma prepare the evening meal of fried chicken, mashed potatoes, corn, and homemade bread.

Rose Marie's job is to sprinkle extra flour on the counter as Momma kneads ingredients into the bread dough.

After kneading is complete, Momma gently places the dough into a bread pan and places a lightweight linen cloth over the dough to protect it from the drafty window air, so it can rise.

"Rose Marie," Momma suggests, "How about if you go outside while the dough is rising and catch a June Bug."

Rose Marie likes to do this. "Yes, Momma. I will. Thank you."

She goes to Momma's sewing machine that sets against a kitchen wall. Above the sewing machine and hammered onto the wall is a spool rack with many colors of thread, as many colors as one can find in the five and dime store.

Rose Marie pulls a green string as tall as she is from one spool. She opens the little wooden drawer in the sewing machine cabinet and retrieves the scissors and cuts the string.

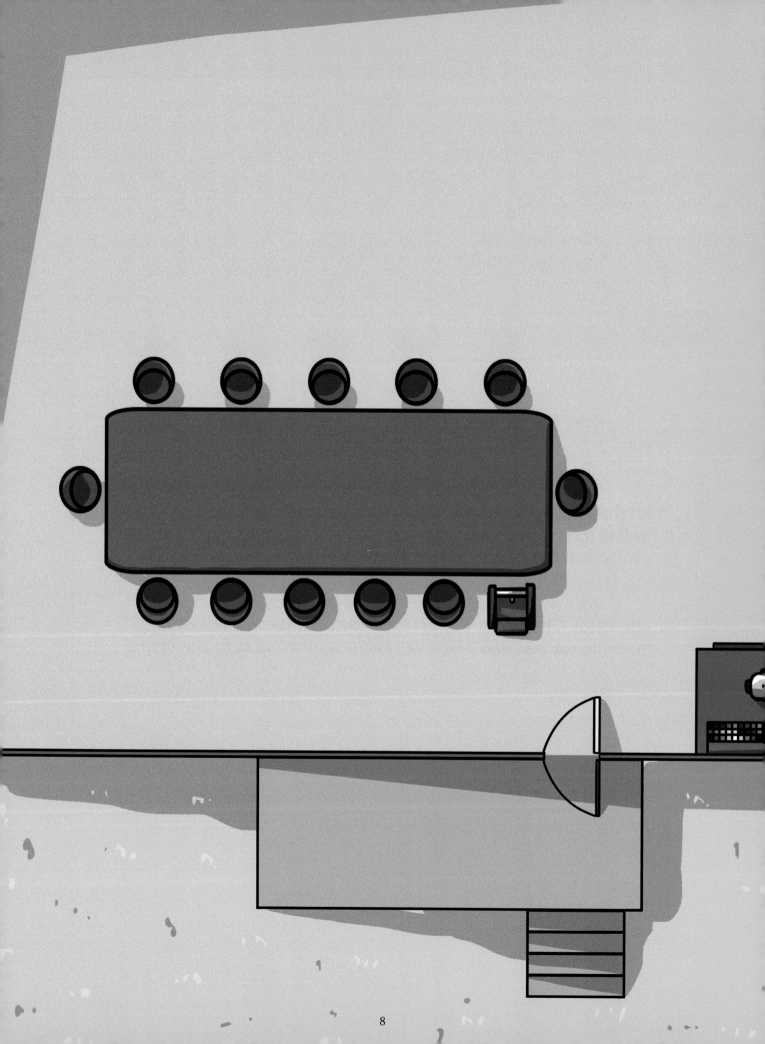

After replacing the scissors, she goes out the back door, down the porch steps, and across the yard to the cellar.

On the grass around the cellar are June Bugs. Rose Marie sits on the grass with crossed legs, searches for the right June Bug, then kindly picks one up.

Gradually, she ties one end of the string onto a hind leg and wraps the other end around her index finger on her right hand. Then, she allows the June Bug to fly around in circles over her head.

As Rose Marie parades through the back yard with June Bug, she hears the jingle of the ice cream truck. She ignores the desire to share in the rhythm of the beat.

June Bug lands on Rose Marie's shoulder and whispers in her ear. "Go find a flat stone in the ditch and hand it to me."

Rose Marie does just this, then places the stone between June Bug's green wings. June Bug rubs the stone between her wings as if you were warming your hands by the fire on a cold wintry day.

Quickly and magically, the stone turns into a quarter. Rose Marie's blue eyes open wide in amazement.

June Bug initiates, "Run. Get yourself an ice cream before the ice cream van rolls away!"

Rose Marie runs towards the ice cream truck. Everyone has already purchased their treats. The truck driver has closed the freezer doors and is about to leave.

Rose Marie shrieks, "Please, sir. Please. Can you re-open the freezer doors? I have a quarter."

The truck driver says, "Sure. What would you like?" Rose Marie purchases a fudgesicle and freezes it to her tongue right away.

"Rose Marie," June Bug invites. "Would you like to eat your ice cream from the top of the world?"

Thinking this might mean flying high on a swing of one of the three swing sets in the backyard, Rose Marie unquestionably exclaims, "Yes, indeed!"

"Well, hang on tight to the string," instructs June Bug.

She wraps the string around her hand and clenches her fingers into a tight fist with all her might.

June Bug yodels, "O-lee-ah-kuh-kee-ya, O-lee-ah-coo-coo. O-lee-ah-kuh-kee-ya, O-lee-ah-coo-coo. O-lee-ah-kuh-kee-ya, O-lee-ah-coo-coo. O-lee-ah-kuh-kee-ya, Goooooo!

Due to amazement, Rose Marie loses her breath. June Bug is taking her to the top of the shady Red Maple tree.

June Bug helps Rose Marie sit on the top of the tree. The leaves are so cool and soft, just like sitting on a fluffy picnic quilt.

June Bug rests on Rose Marie's right shoulder.

Rose Marie eats her fudgesicle and watches the traffic go by. She can see shoppers pushing carts in and out of the grocery store three blocks away.

The newspaper delivery boy rides his bicycle with no hands on the handlebars and throws the papers with accuracy onto the front porches. Mrs. Bell comes out the front door to pick up her paper.

Down Mailbox Way, the postal worker shifts the weight as the envelopes are placed in the mail pack from the drop off box.

Rose Marie's father is up Church Hill mowing the church lawn.

Down Eagle's Way, Mrs. Chattum is sitting under an apple tree in her front yard sorting the Avon orders.

Up Miller Hill, Mr. Asberry puts the leash onto Larry, the huge Rough Collie, and prepares for a walk.

Rose Marie lays back onto the top of the tree and takes in the warm sunshine.

"Rose Marie. Where are you?" Momma is calling.

"June Bug, I need to go. Momma needs me."

June Bug takes Rose Marie down the same way she took her up.

Then and there, Rose Marie takes the string off of June Bug's leg and releases her.

June Bug flies off and is gone in the twinkling of an eye.

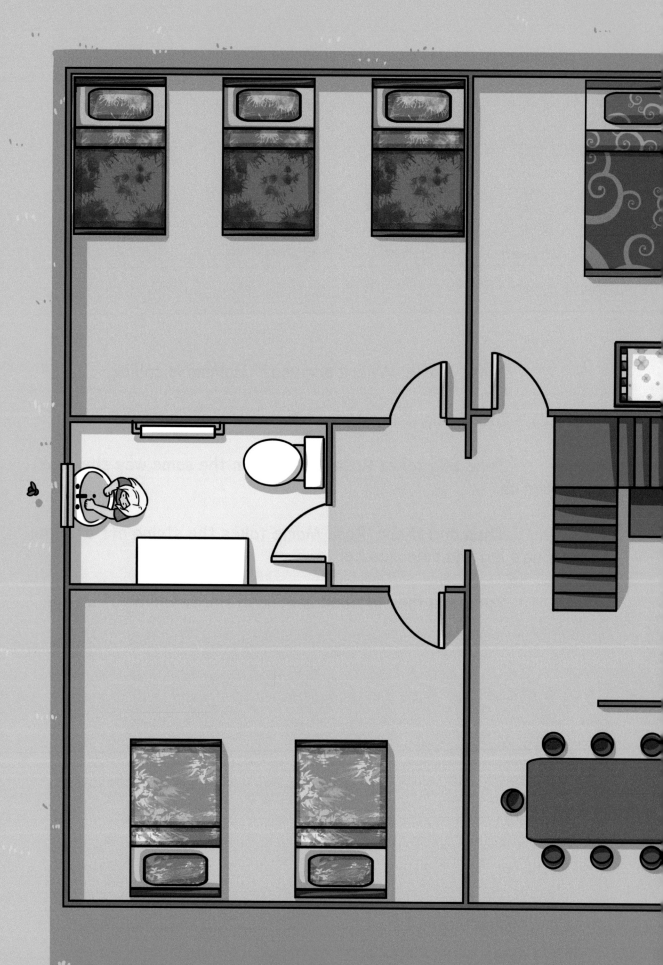

"Rose Marie."

"Coming Momma."

"Did you have a nice time playing?"

"Oh, yes. It was a splendid time, Momma!"

"Well, go and wash up. I need your help."

"It will only take a minute, Momma."

As Rose Marie is washing her hands, she spots June Bug through the bathroom window over the sink.

"Until next time, June Bug. Until next time," Rose Marie whispers.

Printed in the United States
By Bookmasters